PETER PAN

Long ago in London there lived three children—Wendy, John, and Michael.

At bedtime, Wendy told her brothers stories about a faraway place called Never Land. The hero of these stories was Peter Pan, a boy who *never* grew up. Peter's special friend was a tiny fairy called Tinker Bell.

John and Michael loved to act out the stories in which Peter had wonderful adventures.

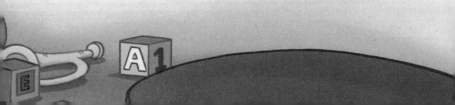

One night, when the children were fast asleep, Peter Pan and Tinker Bell flew in through the nursery window. They had come to search for Peter's shadow. Peter had left it behind one night while he was listening at the window to one of Wendy's stories.

Just then, Wendy woke up. She was thrilled to meet Peter Pan and agreed to help him and Tinker Bell capture the mischievous shadow.

Peter liked Wendy and urged her to fly
with him to Never Land. "You *never* grow
up there!" he promised.

Wendy agreed at once, as long as her
brothers could come, too.

So, Peter told Wendy, John, and Michael
to each think happy thoughts. Then he
sprinkled them with magic pixie dust.

Before they knew it, the excited children
were soaring high above the rooftops of
London.

"Second star to the right and straight on
till morning," Peter called, leading the way.

The children flew all the way to the
enchanted world of Never Land—home
to Peter and the Lost Boys, the dreaded
Captain Hook and his ship of pirates, and . . .

. . . mermaids at the beautiful Mermaid
Lagoon! Wendy and Peter were having
a wonderful time—until . . .

. . . Peter spotted
a little rowboat in
the distance.

"It's Hook, all right!" he cried.

Captain Hook was a wicked pirate and
Peter Pan's greatest enemy.

Once, in a fierce battle, Peter had cut off
Hook's hand. The pirate now had a terrible
steel hook attached to his left wrist.

And where did that hand go?

A hungry crocodile had eaten the pirate's hand! He had enjoyed his meal so much that he now followed Hook everywhere, hoping for a chance to gobble up the rest of him!

Peter and Wendy followed Hook. He
had the Indian Princess Tiger Lily!
"Tell me the hiding place of Peter Pan,
and I shall set you free," Hook snarled.
But Tiger Lily was Peter's friend. She
refused to tell the dastardly pirate!

Peter flew down
in front of Hook just in
the nick of time! Up and down
the rocky cliffs they fought—
until Hook slipped—and the
Croc snapped—hungrily!

Mr. Smee, the Captain's first-mate,
pulled Hook into the rowboat—with the
Crocodile following right behind him.

Peter rescued Tiger Lily and took her home. The Indian Chief made Peter an honorary chief.

At Peter's hideout, Wendy told her
brothers and the Lost Boys a bedtime story.
This made them a little homesick.

"I want my mother," sobbed Michael.

The Lost Boys didn't know what a
mother was, but they decided they wanted
one, too. So, Wendy promised they would
all go back to her London home together.

But Captain Hook and his crew were waiting outside the hideout. The pirates captured the children and took them back to Hook's ship!

Hook gave them a choice: Join the pirates or walk the plank!

The boys rather liked the idea of becoming pirates, but Wendy didn't.

"Peter Pan will save us!" she said.

Hook laughed loudly. "We left a present for Peter—a surprise package." It was a bomb! "Peter will be blasted out of Never Land for*ever*!"

Tinker Bell overheard these words. She had to warn Peter! The tiny fairy reached Peter's hideout just as he was about to open the present.

She grabbed the bomb and threw it
as far away as she could. Seconds later,
there was one *huge* explosion.

Tinker Bell told Peter that Wendy
and the others were in danger, and
Peter sped off to rescue them with
Tinker Bell close behind.

Meanwhile, Hook had forced Wendy to walk the plank. When she stepped off the end of the plank, everybody waited for the SPLASH as she hit the water. But it never came. Peter Pan had arrived just in time to catch her and carry her safely back onto the ship.

Peter Pan then turned to face his enemy.

Peter's dagger and Hook's sword met with a loud clash of steel. Back and forth they went in the most terrible battle ever fought.

High atop the ship's rigging, Hook lunged at Peter. The boy fought back, finally forcing the Captain to slip and fall backward . . .

. . . into the water below, where the hungry Crocodile waited.

The children clapped and cheered as they watched Hook frantically swimming toward Mr. Smee's rowboat, pursued by the snapping jaws of the Croc.

As Hook disappeared into the distance, Peter gave the order to raise the anchor. Tinker Bell sprinkled the pirate ship with magic pixie dust, and in no time at all, the ship was soaring high above Never Land.

The ship flew all the way to London, where Wendy, John, and Michael were soon safely back in their nursery.

As the children waved good-bye, the
pirate ship sailed off into the night sky,
silhouetted against the full moon.